DESERTED

ATTACK ON EARTH

DESERTED

ISRAEL KEATS

darby creek
MINNEAPOLIS

Darby Creek
A division of Lerner Publishing Group, Inc.
241 First Avenue North
Minneapolis, MN 55401 USA

For reading levels and more information, look up this title at
www.lernerbooks.com.

The images in this book are used with the permission of: Bubbledjango/Shutterstock.com; briddy_/iStock/Getty Images; ilobs/iStock/Getty Images; 4khz/DigitalVision Vectors/Getty Images.

Main body text set in Janson Text LT Std 12/17.5.
Typeface provided by Adobe Systems.

Library of Congress Cataloging-in-Publication Data

Names: Keats, Israel, author.
Title: Deserted / Israel Keats.
Description: Minneapolis : Darby Creek, [2018] | Series: Attack on Earth | Summary: Teens Leo, James, and Sigrid are forced to use their instincts to locate their families after an alien invasion disables most electronics and their entire town is evacuated without them.
Identifiers: LCCN 2017056611 (print) | LCCN 2018001735 (ebook) | ISBN 9781541525863 (eb pdf) | ISBN 9781541525740 (lb : alk. paper) | ISBN 9781541526297 (pb : alk. paper)
Subjects: | CYAC: Survival—Fiction. | Extraterrestrial beings—Fiction. | Science fiction.
Classification: LCC PZ7.1.K396 (ebook) | LCC PZ7.1.K396 Des 2018 (print) | DDC [Fic]—dc23

LC record available at https://lccn.loc.gov/2017056611

Manufactured in the United States of America
1-44558-35489-3/20/2018

FOR WILL WEAVER

ON THE MORNING OF FRIDAY, OCTOBER 2, rings of light were seen coming down from the sky in several locations across the planet. By mid-morning, large spacecraft were visible through the clouds, hovering over major cities. The US government, along with others, attempted to make contact, without success.

At 9:48 that morning, the alien ships released an electromagnetic pulse, or EMP, around the world, disabling all electronics—including many vehicles and machines. All forms of communication technology were useless.

Now people could only wait and see what would happen with the "Visitors" next . . .

CHAPTER 1

Today was the day Leo would take the
Death Dive.

Five miles from home, in the middle of
Fuller Woods, was a steep, narrow path that
zigzagged down a big hill. There were tight
turns through the trees, low-hanging branches,
and roots that made for a bumpy ride. The
path ended at the paved bike line that wound
through the woods. The Death Dive wasn't
just riding down the path itself. Leo had
done that dozens of times. The Death Dive
meant sailing down the path at top speed
without stopping.

Leo secretly thought it was kind of a stupid
thing to do, but it was a rite of passage at his

school. His friend Steve had done it ages ago, then Kenny, and finally Joe last Sunday. That meant Leo was the last of his group of friends to do it, and the others kept bugging him about it, asking him when he was going to try. Finally, yesterday, he had blurted out that he would do it today after school.

But he wanted to do a dry run first, so here he was. There was just enough time to do the Dive and get back before his second class. His first class was study hall in the media center, and he figured the librarian wouldn't even notice he wasn't there.

Leo sat at the top of the hill and eyed the path.

He was nervous about wiping out in front of his friends—but the worst that would happen would be them teasing him about it for a few weeks. If he chickened out, everyone at school would know he was a wuss and he'd never live it down.

As he tightened the strap on his helmet, he pictured himself flying down the hill this afternoon. He tried to visualize himself making every turn with ease. Maybe it would even be fun, and he could let loose a little as he took the jumps. He would skid to a stop at the bottom and say, "Piece of cake!" All his friends would cheer for him. Every time he faced a tough test or wanted to ask a girl out he would remember this day.

Leo checked that his backpack's straps were securely buckled across his chest. Then he kicked his way forward. He bit hard into his mouth guard as his front tire dipped. The Death Dive began.

He had to keep his feet pedaling because of the fixed gears, fighting the urge to brake. Though his whole body was tense, he tried to relax and enjoy the Dive. A pine branch whapped his face, but he kept up with the twists and turns of the path.

That pine tree was the halfway point. *Almost there!* he told himself.

The second half of the path wasn't as steep, but it had more obstacles. Leo whipped the bike around a tree, rode out a hard bounce, and hit the bottom of the hill. All he had to do now was keep the bike straight and ride through a narrow gap between two trees, like the posts at a finishing line. He sailed through the trees, letting out a loud whoop. His tire hit the paved bike path and skidded on a patch of gravel. The bike jerked sideways and fell. Leo tumbled to the ground, banging and scraping the left half of his body.

Leo checked his bike: the gear had been hit and bent out of shape. He groaned. He had a small repair kit with him, but nothing that could fix this. He checked himself: the left leg on his jeans was ripped and his left arm was scraped up. Nothing serious, but he had wounds that would impress the others. Maybe some of it would even scar.

He walked the bike to a small patch of dead leaves and leaned it against a tree. He undid the strap under the seat to get his emergency kit. He had alcohol pads to dab the dirt out of his scrapes and an ointment to rub into them. He had bandages too, but this wasn't serious enough for that. Then he turned his attention to the bike itself. He had to push the gear back into place with his bare hands, so he hoped the fix would do for now.

His stomach rumbled. Leo sat down next to his bike and dug through his backpack in search of an energy bar. He tore it open with a frustrated sigh. The wipeout had taken him out of the moment. He was supposed to be celebrating. He'd taken the Death Dive—he'd finally done it!

Leo leaned back against the tree and took a long swig of water from his bottle. As his heart rate slowed, he could feel his limbs grow heavy. *I'll just close my eyes for a few minutes,* he told himself.

***

When his eyes opened again, it took Leo a moment to realize where he was. His neck muscles were sore from the way his chin had been resting on his chest. His back felt numb from sitting on the ground for so long.

School! he thought frantically. *How long was I asleep?* He reached into his pocket for his phone to check the time. The screen was black.

He held down the "On" button to restart it, but nothing happened. Leo turned it over in his hands. The phone must have been damaged in the bike crash.

"Great," he groaned.

Leo stood up and wiped himself off. He'd been out in the woods for longer than he'd planned—probably at least an hour. By the time he got to school, he'd be late for second period, and that teacher would *definitely* notice.

Maybe he could just say he'd wiped out while biking to school. He'd have to limp and groan a lot—act like it was pure suffering to walk into the front office. Show them the broken phone.

He wouldn't have to fake it much, he realized as he got back on the bike and started to pedal.

CHAPTER 2

The gear was still messed up, so the bike was slow to pedal and made a scraping noise as Leo rode. Leo winced every time the metal scraped against metal, but he didn't know what else to do. It would take hours to walk back into town.

The road that led to Fullerton was rarely used, winding through woods and farmland. Dense woodland lined both sides of the road, with a stretch of tall grass between the road and the forest. Leo hoped somebody would come along and offer to give him a ride.

But nobody drove by. Nobody at all.

Leo stopped and looked behind him, then up ahead. The road was empty. He had been biking for about fifteen minutes and not a single vehicle had passed. This area was quiet, but it was unusual for the road to get no traffic at all.

A few minutes later, Leo turned around a bend and saw a truck stopped in the lane. It wasn't even pulled over—it was stopped dead. A big, heavyset man was walking around the truck, waving his arms. As Leo got closer, he heard the man ranting.

"Not a thing works," the man was muttering to himself. "What is going on?"

He finally noticed Leo. "Hey!" he slapped on a friendly smile. "I'm in a bit of a pickle here. Do you have a working phone?"

Leo shook his head. "Mine is dead." He dropped his feet to the ground but stayed seated on the bike.

"Figures," the guy said. "Can't get the truck started or my phone to work."

Leo thought back to the black screen of his own phone. "That's kind of weird," he said. "What are the odds of that?" He looked up at the power lines along the highway, as if they might have the answers.

The man gave him a surprised look. "Haven't you been paying attention to the news?"

Leo shook his head.

"All morning they've been talking about the lights in the sky," the man continued. "Just before everything quit on me, they said on the radio there were weird ships above the clouds. Visitors. From another planet."

"Wait . . . seriously?"

"It was on every news station all morning," the man said. "You really haven't heard anything about it?"

"Uh . . . no." Leo had been so focused on sneaking out early that morning that he hadn't bothered to check social media on his phone.

"Well, listen, how about you loan me that bike?" The man suddenly took a nicer tone. "I can ride up into town, be back with help in . . . what is it from here, a few miles?"

"About four miles," Leo told him, guessing how far he'd biked already. "But I'm keeping the bike. I could send help for you when I get to town."

"Sure you will," the man said. "But, the thing is, I have to call this in myself. I need somebody from my company. Most tow trucks won't be able to get through our security system."

"Well, sorry, then," Leo said. His bicycle was his most valued possession. There was no way he'd let a stranger have it. Not even if it was the end of the world. "Hope someone else comes along."

The man pulled out a handful of bills from his wallet. "How about a hundred bucks? The bike isn't even worth that much. And I'm just renting it. Not buying it."

Leo shook his head. His bike was worth way more than that, but that was beside the point. "It's not for sale. Look, I'm late for school. I have to go—"

"How about you at least let me have a drink of water? I've been out here all morning."

Leo did have a little water left. He climbed off his bike and took the bottle from its holder on the frame. He tossed it over. The man took a long drink, and for a moment, Leo thought about just leaving. The guy could keep the water bottle.

Then the man popped the cap back onto the bottle. "Thanks," he said. He walked over to hand Leo the bottle, standing in front of Leo's bike.

Leo reached out to take the bottle, when suddenly the man tossed it at him and lunged for the bike handles. Leo clutched at his bike as the man tried to jerk the handlebars out of his grip.

"You give me that bike now!"

CHAPTER 3

Leo staggered backward as the man swung a fist at him. The man grabbed at the bike with one hand, still swinging his other fist. Leo ducked forward and held onto the frame of his bike, keeping his head low.

He'd never be able to take this guy if it came to an all-out fight. He'd never be able to wrestle the bike away, and even if he did, he didn't know if he could ride away with the man chasing after him. His mind raced as he tried to figure out what to do.

Suddenly there was a *whop* sound, and the man stumbled backward. He rubbed at his head in confusion.

"What did you do to me?" the man groaned.

The same noise sounded again. A stone whapped the man in the shoulder. The trucker looked past Leo, his eyes wide. While he was distracted, Leo leaped on his bike and kicked off to give himself a burst of speed. He pedaled frantically.

"Hey!" The man reached for him, but Leo twisted the bike away and pedaled hard. The man chased after him for a long terrible minute before he seemed to finally give up, doubling over. Leo biked down the road until he couldn't see the man anymore and stopped to catch his breath.

He heard a noise in the trees lining the highway. Leo tensed, worried the man had somehow sneaked through the woods to come after him again. But then he saw the front tire of a bike roll through the trees.

The bike came to a stop and the rider took off his helmet. It was a boy with long hair, younger than him by maybe a year. "Hey," the boy said. "You okay?"

"Was that you?" Leo asked, waving a hand back in the direction he came from.

The kid nodded and reached into his pocket and pulled out a handmade slingshot. "Looked like he was giving you some trouble."

"He was trying to steal my bike," Leo explained. "It was so weird. He kept talking about . . ." He stopped, not wanting to think about it any longer. "Well, thanks anyway."

"No problem."

Leo glanced down at the kid's bike. "Heading into town?"

"Yeah," the kid said. "I was at home playing video games when the power went out and my phone stopped working. My mom works in town, so I thought I'd try to find her."

Leo raised his eyebrows. It was Friday morning—what was he doing playing video games at home?

"Don't you go to school?"

"Yeah. I'm a freshman at Fullerton High," the kid said, pointing his thumb toward town. "But . . . it's not going so great for me. I just needed a day at home. And now all this weird stuff with the power is happening."

Leo nodded. He remembered freshman year being difficult for some people to adjust to. "Well, hey," he said, "how about I ride back into town with you? I'm Leo."

"James."

They took off down the road together. At first they kept to the shoulder, but after not spotting another car for thirty minutes they drifted to ride in the middle of the road.

"So why aren't *you* in school?" James asked.

Leo felt his face heat up. "Well, I only meant to skip one class. Then my bike got wrecked, so it's been slow. But I'm on my way back to school now."

When they rode into the edge of the city, things still seemed . . . off. The town was still. Apparently every building had lost power— even the stoplights were dead. Cars had been abandoned in the middle of the street.

"So the power's out, but why are all the cars stalled?" Leo asked.

"I don't know," James admitted.

As they hit the center of town, they realized something else.

"Not only is everything out, everyone's *gone*," James said.

"Maybe they're at work," Leo said. "It *is* the middle of the day." He looked around, expecting to see *one* person he could point out. But he didn't. Usually there were some people out and about during the day. People walking dogs, or stay-at-home parents pushing strollers. Delivery trucks driving around. This was the most deserted he'd ever seen the town.

They biked past the main street. It looked as if all the stores were closed. More cars were stopped and empty in the middle of the street.

"Maybe everyone went home after the power went out," Leo suggested.

"You just said you thought they were at work," James said.

Leo let out a huff of breath. "I don't know, man. My parents will be at home either way. They own a restaurant, and they won't open up till later this afternoon. Let's go ask them what's going on."

"Fine. Then we can check on my mom," said James.

A few blocks later they passed by the high school.

"The school looks empty too," James said. They glanced at each other before silently agreeing to check it out. They turned into the bus lane in front of the school.

They left their bikes by the racks, which were still full of locked bikes. Inside the halls were empty and the classrooms silent. The floor was littered with papers and pens and other dropped items.

"Looks like everyone left in a hurry," said James. They walked down the main hall, looking in the empty classrooms. Doors hung open. In one room, tests were left incomplete on the desks.

"They must have sent everybody home," Leo said.

"And given them, like, thirty seconds to get out?" James asked.

"Maybe there was some kind of emergency?" Leo thought back to what the truck driver had said about the Visitors. He'd thought the man was making things up, but now he wasn't sure. He pushed the thoughts out of his head. There had to be a better explanation.

"Come on," he said, walking back toward the front doors. "My parents will tell us what's going on."

They went outside and returned to where they'd left their bikes.

"This way," said Leo, kicking off and pedaling. Though he still didn't know what was going on, he found himself feeling more and more desperate to find his parents. When they arrived at his house, he practically leaped off his bike in the driveway and left it lying there.

Leo ran inside. "Mom? Dad?"

There was no response. The house had never felt emptier.

He walked through the living room and glanced down the hall into his parents' room. The drawers were open, piles of clothes on the bed. They had packed and left in a hurry.

Leo walked to his own room and saw more open drawers. Some of his things were dropped to the floor. So they had packed things for him too, but where did they go? He returned to the living room, where James was waiting.

"Nobody's home?" James asked.

"No. It looks like my folks packed up their stuff. Mine too."

"Yeah, I guessed that."

"But where did they go? And why wouldn't they wait for me?" Leo wondered. "I mean, it's just not like them. If they had to leave, they'd wait for me to get home."

"They thought you were at school," James reminded him. "They probably figured you were evacuated with the rest of the students."

Leo groaned. He immediately regretted skipping class this morning. "Of course they did." He slumped down into a chair. "So we don't know *why* anyone left, and we don't know *where* they went. What now?"

"Let's try to find my mom. I bet she can tell us where they sent everyone."

"What makes you think she's even still there?"

"She probably is," said James. "She's an engineer at DPI. Even if they were evacuating the whole town, I'm guessing people working there would have stayed around."

Leo nodded. DPI was pretty much the largest company in Fullerton. It was an energy company that provided jobs for most people in town. He figured James was right—if anyone was going to stick around to learn more about what had happened to the electricity, it was probably the people at DPI.

Leo and James rode through the empty streets, weaving around the stalled cars, looking for any signs of life. The DPI buildings were on the north end of town surrounded by security fences. They reached the gate and pushed the buttons on the intercom, but none of them worked.

"It must have gotten knocked out with the power," Leo said.

"You'd think they would have a backup generator," James said. "Or at least a way to open the gate by hand."

"Well, if they do I don't know what it is." Leo shielded his eyes against the sun and stared at the building. The parking lot was still filled with cars. "Maybe everyone is locked in there, but it sure looks empty inside."

"Let's go in and look through the front door." James eyed the fence. It was lined with barbed wire.

"We can't climb over that," Leo said.

"Nope," James agreed. He grasped the gate with both hands and shook, making it rattle. "There's no way they didn't leave a single security guard behind." He started shouting. "Hey! Is anyone there?" There was no response.

James gave up. "Seems like they could have at least put up a sign. Even if my mom *is* in there, I have no way of letting her know I'm out here." He shook his head. "This is so weird."

"Let's ride back to my place," Leo suggested. "Maybe my parents will be coming back—maybe they were just out looking for me."

The look James gave him told Leo that he didn't believe that, but he didn't seem to have any other ideas. "Sure, okay," he said finally.

He gave one more disappointed glance toward the DPI buildings.

They rode back on side streets, past dark houses and buildings. Even the police station looked closed. If the police station was closed, what could be open?

Leo looked at the familiar red bulb at the top of the town's water tower. He was so used to seeing it, he usually didn't even notice it. He braked and James stopped behind him.

"What is it?" James asked.

"I have an idea."

CHAPTER 4

They left their bikes near the tower and walked over. The lower part of the ladder was in a metal tube-like cage, which was locked. But the legs of the water tower had smaller crisscrossing beams to support them.

"So, how do we get up?" James asked.

"Watch."

Leo leaped up and grabbed the lowest crossbar. He let himself swing for a moment, hoping it looked like he was just gathering momentum. In reality, Leo had never done this before. He'd heard of kids at school doing it before, and some of his friends claimed they'd done it. So in theory he knew what to do.

As his legs began swinging higher, he hoped to himself that it was as easy everyone else made it seem. He swung his feet to the crossbar and locked his ankles around it, then shifted his hands and feet until he reached one of the water tower's large legs. The bar ran up at an angle. He reached up for the next cross bar, which angled the other way. He went hand over hand again until he reached the platform. He clambered over the railing and took a deep breath.

He looked down and saw James was already halfway up. He was also breathing hard when he reached the platform. Leo flexed his hands. The narrow crossbars were hard on the palms.

"How many kids have died doing this?" James asked.

"None that I know of," Leo said. "But I heard about one guy who broke an ankle."

"If that happened to us, we'd have no way to call for help," said James.

"I guess not," Leo admitted. "But look, we can see most of the town from here."

There was the blue roof of the pizza restaurant his parents owned, and just down the street was the playground he'd played at as a kid. Both were usually busy this time of day, but now there were no signs of life at either one.

"It's a ghost town," said James.

"Yeah," Leo said quietly. Then he noticed movement out of the corner of his eye.

His gaze darted to a house just a few blocks away from his own. The yard had a high wooden privacy fence around it, but from up here they could see right in. The blinds were drawn closed in most of the windows, but in one of them on the lower level he could see there was a dark gap in the blinds. He watched it for a moment, and then suddenly the blinds snapped closed.

"Look!" He pointed.

"What?"

"I just saw someone looking through those blinds. Someone's there!"

"I still don't see—" James stopped when the side door to the house quickly opened.

A yellow pit bull came bounding over from the backyard and scurried into the house. A girl poked her head out, glancing around the yard. Then she yanked the door closed behind her.

"Sigrid," Leo said in surprise.

James looked at him. "You know her?"

He nodded. "Sort of. She goes to our school. We used to ride the same bus when we were kids."

"Let's go talk to her," James said. "She might know something." Then he hesitated. "I don't suppose there's an easier way down?"

"Not unless you have a parachute," said Leo. He started back down the same way they came.

"Ugh." James followed.

They made it safely to the ground and biked over to the house. Leo's heart was beating quickly. He never thought he'd be this excited to see a girl he barely knew.

Leo punched the doorbell, then realized it probably didn't work. He rapped on the door. There was no answer.

"Sigrid! It's Leo," he called. Then he realized she may not recognize his name. "From school," he added lamely. Inside the dog started barking.

"It's okay, Sandy," they heard a girl's voice say through the door. The door cracked open, and Sigrid looked out at him in surprise.

"Uh, hey," he said. "I'm Leo. We go to school together. And this is James." He pointed over his shoulder with his thumb. "He goes there too."

She continued to stare at them, clearly wondering why they were standing at her front door.

Leo cleared his throat. "So listen, do you . . . know where everyone went? I went for a ride in the woods this morning, and when I got back everyone was gone or something. Everybody except you."

Her eyebrows narrowed. "You don't know?"

"Know what?"

"Just come inside," she said, rolling her eyes. She opened the door and let them in, shutting and locking it behind them. The pit bull—Sandy, Leo figured—followed them into the dining room.

"The army evacuated the entire town after the power went out," Sigrid explained as she sat down at the table. "They gathered everyone at the schools and loaded them up in transport trucks. They didn't even give people a chance to go home first—said there was no time."

"How is it their vehicles work when all the others are stalled?" Leo wondered.

"I don't know," Sigrid said.

"They're the military," James said. "Of course they have the best technology to withstand anything."

"That would make sense," Sigrid said. "After the Visitors attacked—"

Leo's eyes widened. "The . . . Visitors?" he repeated. "That's actually, like, a thing?"

"What are you talking about?" asked James, who was clearly even more confused than Leo.

"That guy who tried to steal my bike earlier mentioned something about 'Visitors' too. I thought he was just trying to mess with me."

"Wait," James said, looking back and forth between Sigrid and Leo. "Who are the Visitors?"

Sigrid sighed and gestured to the chairs across from her. "You guys had better sit down."

CHAPTER 5

"Early this morning there were these . . .
lights in the sky," Sigrid explained. "Like
rings. And then the news said there were
spaceships. Aliens. Everyone's been calling
them the Visitors."

Leo couldn't believe it. The guy on the
highway had been right.

"But before they could say much else,
everything got zapped," Sigrid continued. "No
power, no telephones, nothing. I heard one
army guy call it an EMP—electromagnetic
pulse." She shook her head. "How could you
not know about this? It's all everyone was
talking about at school today."

"Neither of us were there this morning,"

Leo said. He looked over and saw James staring down at his knees.

"I was playing video games all morning. My mom kept calling me, and I didn't feel like answering. She was trying to tell me." James clenched his fists. "Do you know if they evacuated DPI too?"

"I mean, it sounded like they were making everybody leave," said Sigrid. "They might have cleared our town *because* of the DPI buildings. Who knows what kind of stuff they've got going on in there. Maybe they thought the EMP made it risky."

"I should have answered the phone." James sighed. "She would have told me what to do. And she probably left a voicemail, but I can't even check it now. I'm an idiot!"

"You didn't know," Leo said. That didn't seem to bring James much comfort. Leo tried to change the subject. "If they were evacuating everyone at the schools, why did you come home?" he asked Sigrid.

"Because of Sandy." She reached down and rubbed Sandy's ears. "I couldn't stand the thought of leaving her. I live with my grandparents, and they both teach at the elementary school. I knew they'd be with those kids in the transport. Everyone was panicking at the school, so I sneaked out an emergency exit. I thought I could get Sandy and bring her back with me in time, but when I got back to the school the transports had already left. I would have gone after them, but I didn't exactly want to go by myself. I've been sticking around here until I can figure out what to do next."

"How long until everyone comes back?" James asked.

She shrugged. "They didn't say."

"Do you know where they went?"

"Actually, yes," she said, perking up. "The old Air Force base."

"That's a long way away," said James.

"Well, yeah. That's why I haven't tried to head there on my own."

Leo sighed. "So we can either try to make our way to the Air Force base with no idea of how to get there and no GPS, or we can stay in town and hope everyone comes back soon." He looked at James. "What do you want to do?"

Sigrid watched quietly as both boys thought it over.

"Well," James said eventually, "we don't know when everyone will be back. For all we know they're already on their way home."

"That's true," Sigrid said.

"And," he continued, "what if we leave right as they're coming back? We might take a different route and pass them completely."

"Then we'd be stuck at the Air Force base by ourselves. Back to square one," Leo added. "So . . . we wait it out here? At least for a few days?"

James nodded, and they both looked to Sigrid, who leaned back in her chair. "Well, you both know my plan was already to stay put. You guys could stay here with me if you want. Our kitchen is pretty well-stocked with food."

"My house is outside of town," James said. "I'd rather stay here."

"Yeah, okay," Leo agreed. "Beats being home alone." He smiled at Sandy, who crossed through the room. "And at least we have a guard dog here."

Sigrid grinned. "Best guard dog around."

All three were quiet for a moment, glancing around the room. Leo noticed Sigrid's fingers tapping against the table, and he wondered if she was missing the habit of checking her phone as much as he was.

"Well," James said. "We're the only ones left in town. I say we make the most of it."

Leo was about to say something in agreement when they heard James's stomach growl loudly. His face flushed red, and he gave them a sheepish smile.

Sigrid laughed softly. "How about we raid my kitchen first?"

CHAPTER 6

After they'd eaten their fill of what they could find in Sigrid's cabinets, they decided to wander through town. They walked through the streets, checking the buildings for any sign of people.

"Nothing," James called from where he was peering into a dark coffee shop window. He joined Sigrid and Leo where they were standing in the middle of the street. Sandy was with them too, sniffing along the curb as they walked. "You know, this is kind of cool."

Sigrid raised her eyebrows at him. "We've been abandoned in the middle of an alien invasion and you think this is *cool?*"

"Well, obviously not that part, but . . . you know what I mean." James moved to stand in the middle of an intersection. "Usually at this time of day this street is packed with cars. Now, it's like the town is ours."

"Yeah, I get it," Leo said. "No parents around, no teachers. Even having no phones or TVs or anything . . . it's different. It feels like the world is on pause."

They wandered through the high school again, this time taking their time. They checked out the teachers' lounge—decidedly not as interesting as the three of them had thought it would be—and climbed up into the rafters of the auditorium just because they could. They spent about an hour shooting hoops in the gym.

After they were done at the school, they circled through the streets back to Sigrid's house. It was a small town, so there wasn't much to explore.

As they rounded a corner, they heard a crash coming from up the street. They froze. Sandy must have heard it too—she bared her teeth and began growling lowly. Sigrid tried to shush her.

Two men were standing in front of an electronics store down the street. One of them had wound a jacket around his fist and had punched it through the glass window. The other one hoisted a stuffed backpack over his shoulder. As he moved, his shirt shifted to reveal a gun tucked into his jeans. The first guy cleared the glass away to unlock the door, letting them in. A bell jingled as the door swung open, and Leo was half expecting to hear the shrill sound of an alarm.

"Easy girl," Sigrid whispered to Sandy, who was still growling. Leo didn't blame her—the guys looked like bad news.

The men were still inside the building and didn't seem to have noticed them. Leo grabbed James and Sigrid by the arms, pulling them backward with him. "Let's take a different route back," he said. He figured the looters were more interested in grabbing things than having any kind of confrontation, but he wasn't about to find out.

Sigrid looked shaky as she nodded in agreement. They crept across the intersection to keep moving down the street they'd come from. Sandy followed closely behind but didn't make a sound. Leo was thankful—he didn't know what he would do if they ran into some bad company like that.

***

They got back to Sigrid's house as the sun began to set. Though no one had said anything, Leo could tell the others felt just as spooked by the looters as he had. Without discussing, they all made sure the doors and windows to the house were locked. They pulled blinds and curtains closed and tossed towels over windows that didn't have coverings.

Dinner was another round of searching the pantry shelves for anything that didn't need to be cooked to be eaten. This meal was noticeably less fun and carefree as their lunch had been. Leo felt foolish now for thinking the three of them were the only people left in the entire town. And it certainly hadn't occurred to him till now that anyone left might not have the best intentions.

He tried to remind himself that staying here was still the right idea. *We don't know what's out there*, he told himself as he chewed on a granola bar. *There could be more people like that out in the woods. At least we're safe here in the house.*

Sigrid got up to pour some dog food into Sandy's bowl. Since none of the water worked in the house anymore, she'd brought in a pack of water bottles from the garage. She was pouring a bottle into Sandy's water dish when they heard another crash of glass in the distance. She jumped, spilling water all over the floor.

Leo and James locked eyes, frozen in place. Leo felt his heart pound in his chest. The broken glass wasn't in Sigrid's house, but it had been close.

They rushed to the front window, each of them peering out through the blinds. The setting sun had cast long shadows across the fronts of the houses across the street. Leo couldn't see much.

"There!" James whispered, pointing to the right.

Leo moved to a different window where he could get a better view. Sure enough, the same looters were breaking into a front door two houses down across the street. He noticed the house next to that one also had broken glass in the door. "Looks like they're making their way down that side of the street," he said. "It's getting dark—they'll probably quit for the night soon."

"What if they have some kind of lights?" Sigrid whispered.

"I can barely see as it is. If they had lights, they'd be using them already." It wasn't the most convincing argument, but it was all they had to go with.

Sigrid and James nodded, but Leo could tell no one felt reassured. As the sun went down, they lit a few candles and kept them away from the windows to be safe. Sigrid brought down armfuls of pillows and blankets into the living room for the three of them to sleep. Leo dragged a recliner over to the front door, propping it between the door and the staircase. James and Sigrid moved the kitchen table to block the side door.

Leo could feel that something among them had shifted. This place no longer seemed as safe as they'd thought it would be. He cleared his throat, and the other two turned to him. "I, uh, wonder if we should leave for the Air Force base tomorrow morning after all."

James nodded, looking relieved. "How far away is the base?"

"They said it would be over an hour in the transport vehicles," said Sigrid. "So maybe seventy, eighty miles west?"

"If we make good time, we could probably get there within a day on bikes," Leo said. He looked at Sigrid. "Do you have a bike?"

"Yeah, but I also have a dog," she reminded them. "I'm not leaving her behind."

"How about one of those little trailers that you can tow behind a bike?" James suggested. "They look like tents? Usually people put little kids in them?"

"Great idea." Sigrid snapped her fingers.

"I know where I can get one. A family I babysit for has one. I have a key to their house, and I know the mom wouldn't mind if I borrowed it."

"All right," Leo said. "We'll leave first thing tomorrow morning." He felt better knowing what they were going to do next, even if it was riding bikes for eight or nine hours while towing an elderly dog.

They spent the rest of the evening getting ready for the trip. Sigrid emptied her backpack of her schoolbooks and found extra bags for Leo and James. Leo stuffed one backpack full of energy bars and peanut butter sandwiches. He saw James putting cans of soda in another.

"You know that's going to be warm. And not very, like, nutritious or whatever."

James looked at him and blinked. "You're right. I hadn't thought about that." He put the cans on the counter and loaded the water bottles instead.

After they were finished, they sat in the nest of blankets and pillows in the living room—Sigrid on the couch, James and Leo on the floor.

"I've been wondering," James said. "Why us?"

Sigrid shifted to lie down on the couch. "Why Earth?"

"Yeah."

"Maybe they know we're the only other planet out there with life," she suggested.

"But what are the odds that only two planets in the entire universe have life?" Leo asked. "I feel like if we know there are at least two out there, that just means there's probably more."

"And why attack us?" Sigrid asked.

"I mean, can we really even call it an attack?" said James. "It's not like they bombed us."

Sigrid snorted. "Nope, just wiped out our means of transportation and communication."

"But they might have just wanted to neutralize us. Doesn't seem like they're out to destroy us."

"How comforting."

"Well, James is right that it could've been worse," said Leo, shrugging. "And for all we know, they might be talking with the government right now, coming up with some sort of peaceful compromise. It's not like we'd hear about it in our newsfeeds anymore anyway."

The candles went out, and with nothing else to do they decided to go to sleep. It was strange, Leo thought to himself as he stared up at the ceiling, with the power being knocked out noises in the house seemed even louder than usual. They all jumped any time the wind caused a tree branch to scratch on the roof.

At one point in the middle of the night, the house creaked as it shifted. Sigrid had yelped in surprise, and Leo felt his heart pounding in his chest.

Even though he was with two other people, Leo realized that without technology to help them learn what was going on, he felt entirely alone.

CHAPTER 7

Leo tossed and turned all night. He'd barely get into a light sleep before he'd think he heard something—Visitors or looters alike—outside. They didn't have any sort of alarm set, but all three managed to wake up around sunrise.

They each grabbed a box of cereal from Sigrid's pantry. They didn't trust the milk in the fridge, so they ate it dry. When they were finished, they quietly crept around the house, grabbing their bags and any other last-minute supplies they could think of. James and Leo found Sigrid in the driveway, attaching the trailer to her bike.

After she helped Sandy into the trailer and

hooked a helmet on her head, Sigrid turned to them. "Ready?"

Leo nodded, trying to give a brave face.

James just snorted. "No, but I'd rather try our luck out there than stay around here." He kicked off and started pedaling. "Let's do this."

The morning air was damp and cold as they set out. Leo knew it would be a long day, but he figured they would get to the base before dark, even while towing a dog. Sigrid had left the trailer's window flap open and Sandy's snout poked out, sniffing the air.

They reached the edge of town in a few minutes. James—riding in front of the group—skidded to a halt. "Oh no."

Leo caught up and saw what he meant. Down the road was a row of barricades dragged into the middle of the highway. A couple men stood there as if they were guarding it.

"Maybe they're police or army officers," Leo said. "We could turn ourselves in."

"Turn ourselves in? We're not criminals," said James.

"You know what I mean," said Leo. "We could tell them we were left behind and they would get us to that Air Force base."

"We don't know who they are though," Sigrid pointed out. "They're not wearing any uniforms. They could be looters too. What if the only people left are the bad ones?"

"*We're* still here, aren't we?" Leo said. Sigrid opened her mouth and he knew she was about to tell him that was different. "We could at least go closer and see," he added.

James shook his head. "I don't know. Sigrid is right—we don't know who those guys are. Once they see us we can't back out."

"I'd rather go it alone for a while," said Sigrid. "Unless we find someone wearing a uniform."

"Fine," said Leo. "But we'll have to go off-road if we want to avoid people." He turned his bike and started doubling back. "I know where we can get on a trail. It ends just out of town, but will get us past the barricade."

They rode easily on the paved trail, but it ended in a mess of thick bushes and rocky ground. Leo's bike was designed for hard riding, but both James and Sigrid had trouble riding over the uneven and rocky ground with their street bikes. Sigrid had it the worst with the dog trailer dragging behind her.

As they neared the barricade, only a few rows of trees and brush between them and the other group, Leo waved his hand for everybody to be silent. They got past the barricade, and Leo let out his breath.

They rode a half mile or so further, afraid to come out where they might be seen. Leo turned to say something to the others when he noticed rustling in the trees in front of them.

They froze. A group of men stepped out. They didn't look like police officers, and they didn't look like they were offering help. Sandy rumbled a low growl from the trailer.

"What are you kids doing out here?" one asked.

"We live in town," Leo said, gesturing behind him to where they'd come from. "We got left behind in the evacuation. We're just trying to catch up with everyone—we don't want any trouble."

The man raised his eyebrows at the word *trouble*.

"We're setting up camp over near the lake," he said. "We're going to wait out this thing." Leo noticed there was still a tag dangling from his knife case. In fact, all of their shirts and hats looked new too. He wondered if these guys had let themselves into a sporting goods store and loaded up on gear.

One of the men was eyeing the backpacks the three were wearing. Leo knew if they gave up their supplies, they'd have a much harder time of getting to the Air Force base.

"What's in the bags?"

"Just some food," said Sigrid. "Nothing valuable."

"Well, if you share your food, we'll share our site. How about that?" the man said.

"We're passing through," Leo said. "That's all."

"Well, share a little breakfast with us, then you can be on your way."

"We need it," Sigrid said, her voice firm. "We don't have much."

"Unloading some of that food and water might lighten up your packs, make your ride a little easier," another guy said. He took a step toward them, and Sandy's growls rose in volume.

"We said no," Sigrid continued.

The man lurched toward her. "Now, you listen—"

There was a ripping sound as Sandy plunged through the window of the tent, tearing through the Velcro. She leaped in front of Sigrid and bared her teeth as she growled.

The men hesitated, looking at one another. It gave the opportunity Leo was waiting for. "Run!" he shouted to his friends.

He and James took off, dragging their bikes beside them until they were able to hop on. Leo noticed Sigrid still stood beside her bike, watching Sandy. "Sigrid, come on!" he hissed.

She looked back at Sandy, who was still growling at the men, one more time before climbing onto her bike and following after Leo and James. They pedaled through the trees as quickly as they could. Behind them, Leo could hear Sandy's growls turning into deep barks. He hoped she would keep the men at bay in time for them to get some distance.

But as they reached the highway and Leo hopped onto his bike, the devastated look on Sigrid's face made his stomach twist with guilt.

CHAPTER 8

The riding was hard, but they managed to stay just ahead of the men. Without the weight of a dog, the trailer twisted and bounced lightly behind Sigrid's bike. They kept riding until they couldn't hear the men tumbling after them through the brush. The sounds of Sandy's barks faded away too.

Finally, Leo slowed when he couldn't feel his legs anymore. The others paused too. They perched on their bikes as they struggled to catch their breath.

"Jeez, is everyone that's left around here a huge jerk?" James asked, panting.

Leo was about to respond when he noticed Sigrid. She was watching the tree lines with a worried look on her face. "Hey," he said, "she'll be okay. She'll find us."

"I can't believe I just left her," Sigrid said with a weak voice.

James walked his bike over to her and placed a hand on her shoulder. "She wanted to protect us—we did what we had to."

Leo could tell that Sigrid wouldn't want to keep going without Sandy, and his legs still felt like jelly from the hard ride. "Let's take a break," he suggested. "We can keep an eye out for her."

Sigrid looked at him thankfully. "Yeah," she said. "Okay."

They wheeled their bikes over to the line of trees, hoping to stay out of sight for that other group but still visible enough for Sandy to spot them if she came after them.

After ten minutes with no sign of her, Leo began to get worried. He knew they could only wait for Sandy for so long, and he didn't know how he was going to be able to convince Sigrid to leave without her.

Just as Leo was working up the nerve to tell Sigrid they should start thinking about leaving, they heard a familiar bark in the distance. They stood up to see Sandy trotting down the highway. She'd spotted them, and as she came closer she wagged her tail.

"Oh my god," Sigrid cried. "I can't believe it!" She wrapped her arms around Sandy as the dog bounded over to her.

"Good girl!" Sigrid said. She checked over Sandy's body. "She's perfectly fine. But ugh, you're wet, Sandy!" She pushed the dog down. Leo saw—and smelled—that she was right. Sandy was soaked, and her paws and legs were covered with mud.

Sigrid rubbed her hands along Sandy's back. "She's freezing. We have to warm her up."

"We should build a fire," James said. "Get her dry and warm."

"With what?"

"Wood?" He pointed out some fallen branches.

"I mean how do we start the fire? I don't have any matches. Do you?"

"Nope, but we'll figure it out. Rubbing sticks together or whatever."

They walked their bikes into the woods until they found a small clearing that had good tree coverage. James volunteered to gather wood while Sigrid tried to clean up the dog and Leo sorted through his backpack for some food. After he'd collected a small pile, James pulled the bark off of two branches and started sawing at one with the other. Nothing happened.

"Guess it's harder than I thought," he said. "Usually I'd just look for a video online to show me how to do this."

Sigrid looked over at him. "Shouldn't you build, like, a fire pit or something first anyway?"

Leo laughed when James looked down at the grass he was kneeling in. It looked like he had planned on starting the fire right in the middle of the ground. James sat back on his heels and sighed. "Man, I always thought this kind of thing would be so easy. They sure make it look like it in the movies."

"Yeah, and it's not like they teach *this* kind of thing in school," Leo said.

Sigrid pulled out a sweatshirt from her backpack and used it to dry off Sandy's fur.

"Well, at least I brought two of these. Guess one of them is yours now, girl!"

"So we don't have a fire," James said. "At least we have food. I'm starving—can we eat now?"

"Um . . ." Leo said, looking at what was in his backpack. "Sure. Sort of." He pulled out one of the peanut butter sandwiches— it was squished inside the plastic bag. His backpack had gotten more jostled than he'd expected. The crackers had been crushed into crumbs.

"Well, this is for lunch," he said, passing out a crumbling sandwich to James and Sigrid. They ate as best they could, scraping the food out of the bags and pouring crumbs into their mouths. They washed it down with lukewarm water.

"We are really bad at surviving," said James.

"Yeah. Well, once this food is gone it'll get harder," said Leo. "We'll have to hunt. Or gather. Or whatever."

A brisk wind picked up as they pushed Sandy back into her tent. Sigrid had wrapped

her up in the sweatshirt, so she looked like she
had at least gotten a little warmer.

They headed back to the highway and set
out on their way. They passed a few signs for a
wilderness preserve, reminding people to clean
up their litter and be careful with their fires.

Sigrid laughed at that one. "If we can start
a fire, we'll be careful with it," she said.

A couple of hours later they found a small
rest stop. There was a set of bathrooms and
an old-fashioned water pump. They were
surprised to see it still worked. They refilled
their water bottles, and Sigrid found some
paper towels in the bathrooms that she used to
towel off Sandy. At least now she was relatively
clean and dry.

"Here you go, girl," Sigrid said as she
poured out half her water bottle for Sandy
to drink. Leo went back into the rest stop
building to throw away the paper towels, and
he spotted James staring at a bulletin board in
the hall.

Leo walked over to join him and realized
James was looking at a map on the bulletin

board. A red star marked their current location.

"I don't think we've been going fast enough," James said, resting his finger on the red star. "It's already getting dark out—I don't think we're gonna get to the Air Force base tonight. But," he reached for a brochure pinned up on the board, "I found this lodge. Looks like it's not too far away."

The town listed in the brochure looked to be in the same direction as the Air Force base. Leo grabbed it and paged through it. The lodge was a small resort with half a dozen cabins and a main building. On the back of the brochure, he found a miniature map and checked it against the map on the wall—sure enough, they weren't too far away.

"We could stay there for the night," James suggested. "Beats lying on the floor in here. We could at least sleep in a cabin or something."

"Sounds like a plan," said Leo. He pocketed the brochure and pulled the map off the wall as well, tucking it into his backpack.

"Fine by me," said Sigrid, who had walked in to join them. "We might even find a stove. And matches," she quickly added.

But a few minutes after they started in what they hoped was the right direction, they felt wet drops on their backs. They hurried back to the rest stop building and sat under the overhang. It began to pour down rain, so heavy they could hardly see.

"Add a raincoat to the list of things I should have brought," Leo said. "Along with matches and a compass. Next time aliens attack, I'm bringing all those things with me."

"And a towel for the dog," Sigrid added.

"And sleeping bags," James said with a laugh. "Since I think this is where we're sleeping tonight."

They were quiet again for a moment, watching the rain come down in sheets. They sat with their backs against the wall. Sigrid had laid her spare sweatshirt on the ground for Sandy to lie on, and after a few minutes of anxiously barking at the thunder, the dog had finally settled down.

"I've popped a million aliens in games but never thought this would happen for real." James waved his hands at the sky, which was black with clouds.

"I wonder what their planet looks like," Sigrid said. "I wonder what *they* look like. Think they'll be friendly?"

"Why would they fry all of our electronics if they wanted to be friends?" James asked.

"Because they don't want us to lob bombs and ask questions later."

James just shrugged. The fact of the matter was, even if someone out there knew what the Visitors wanted, it wasn't like the rest of the world was going to hear about it any time soon.

The rain kept falling. They ate the last of their smashed sandwiches and cheese with smashed crackers. Eventually they all slept, but the cold woke them up before the sun came out. At least it had stopped raining. They had an energy bar each for breakfast and started out, biking slowly through the mud. James and Sigrid didn't seem interested in talking, which was fine with Leo. Between his hands

numb from the cold and his legs tired from
all the pedaling, he wasn't in the mood for it
either. And while last night they'd spent hours
sharing their thoughts on the Visitors, today
Leo decided that was the last thing he wanted
to think about.

CHAPTER 9

"I think I smell food," James said after they'd been dragging their way through the mud for what felt like hours.

"It's a mirage," Sigrid said.

"Can mirages be smells?"

"I smell it too—someone's cooking," Leo offered. "I wonder if we're close to that campsite."

A few minutes later they heard voices and saw the shapes of buildings through the trees. They came up behind a big lodge where people were milling around outside. It was mostly adults, but there were a few kids running around too.

"There's a lot of people here," Leo said.

"And they're making breakfast."

James stopped his bike, leaning one foot on the ground. He frowned. "I don't know if I trust people anymore."

"But they're making breakfast!" Leo said.

"We can at least check them out," Sigrid said. "From a distance."

Leo didn't know if they could trust anyone else either, but his hunger was bigger than his fear. They started riding toward the wonderful smells. They got off their bikes and leaned them against the cabin, then peered around the side.

"They seem friendly enough," Sigrid said.

"None of them have weapons on them," said Leo. "That's a good sign."

"Uh-oh," said James. "They saw us."

Sure enough a woman was walking their way, waving. "Hiya," she said. "You kids alone?"

"We are for now," Leo told her. "Heading to find our families."

"Do you need something to eat?" the woman asked. Leo didn't need another invitation. He walked over. James followed, and so did Sigrid after she let Sandy out of the trailer. In front of the cabin there were grills going. The picnic tables were full of people.

"Grab a plate!" the woman said, pointing to a stack of paper plates. Leo took one and got in line. Soon his plate was full of food. He grabbed a seat and started eating. The others sat with him, stuffing themselves. Even Sandy got to enjoy some table scraps.

"Thanks for this," Sigrid said as the woman sat down with them.

"We need to use up all this food anyway," she explained.

"Yeah." Leo thought of the food at home going bad, and the food at the restaurant his parents managed. It would normally be a disaster but now seemed like a small problem.

The woman introduced herself as Mary Ellen. They gave her their names, but didn't say where they were from or where they were going. Mary Ellen didn't ask. Leo liked that about her.

"You're welcome to wait things out here," she said. "We'll put you to work, is all."

They could do worse, Leo thought to himself. But he'd have to talk to Sigrid and James privately. "We'll work for our food, for sure," he told her, gesturing to their plates.

After they were full, they helped wash down tables and pick up litter. It was worth a little labor to get a good meal, but Leo wanted to get moving. They still had a long way to go.

"So, are we staying or going?" he whispered to James and Sigrid as they hauled bags to the dumpster.

"Going. I want to find my mom," James said.

"Yeah," Sigrid said, "I'd like to make sure my grandparents are okay."

Leo felt relieved. The people here seemed nice enough, but he knew he'd feel better if he could be with his parents again. "All right," he said. "Let's tell Mary Ellen."

The three of them walked into the cabin where a small group was having a meeting. They had metal folding chairs in a circle in the middle of the main room.

"Hi, kids!" Mary Ellen said cheerfully. "This meeting is closed, but I can talk to you in about fifteen minutes, okay?"

"We just wanted to say thank you again before we head out," Sigrid said.

"We're going to go find our families," Leo added. "But we really appreciate the breakfast."

"Oh no," Mary Ellen said, blinking. "You should stay. We're going to be first, you know."

"First for what?"

"The first to make contact with the Visitors," she said.

"What do you mean?"

"We're working on getting a radio running again," she explained. "We're going to tell the Visitors we're here and excited to see them."

Leo looked at Sigrid and James. What was she talking about?

"It's true," a man added. "When the Visitors get our message, they'll know we're the ones for the first trip to our new home. We'll set an example for everyone else."

"You mean you're waiting for the *aliens* to come and get you?" Sigrid said.

"Sure," said Mary Ellen. "They're going to take us to their home. Which will be *our* home from now on."

"Um. Okay. Great. We'll just go outside and, uh, watch for the Visitors." Leo nodded at the others and they started out. The teens exchanged uneasy glances once they were out of sight. But when they looked up they saw two women blocking the door. They kept the big, friendly smiles plastered across their faces.

"Something tells me our new friends aren't as excited as they should be," one of them said.

CHAPTER 10

"Sure we are," Leo quickly replied. "We hadn't thought of that, but it makes sense."

"Yep." James nodded eagerly. "Can't wait to see our new home."

The woman narrowed her eyes. "Maybe you should wait inside."

James charged for the door, ducking between the two women as they closed in. He slipped by and kicked the door open. He stumbled across the doorway, skidding onto his knees and yelping. One of the women reached for James's shirt and yanked on it. Leo followed after James. He pushed the woman away and grabbed James by the arms, pulling him up. Sigrid was right behind them.

"I don't like shoving people!" Leo hissed as they ran around the lodge and grabbed their bikes.

"You had to!" Sigrid said back.

James limped along with them. Leo could see his jeans had ripped and his knees were a little bloody, but he was keeping up with them just fine.

Sigrid looked for her dog. "Sandy!"

She darted toward them, zipping past the people in the yard. Leo and James got onto their bikes as Sigrid helped Sandy into the bike trailer.

Mary Ellen and another woman caught up with them as Sigrid zipped up the trailer.

"So you're going to run away from salvation!" Mary Ellen shouted.

"I think we'll be okay," said Sigrid, jumping back on her bike. The three of them rode hard without looking back.

Eventually they realized no one was chasing after them, so they stopped to catch their breath. Sandy had whined back in her trailer for the first few minutes they rode, but after a while she had fallen into a deep sleep.

"You okay?" Leo asked James, who was panting.

James nodded. "Just skinned my knees. Not too bad."

Leo climbed off his bike, suddenly thankful for the emergency kit on his bike. "I've got some ointment and bandages. Here," he said. He handed them over to James, who sat on the ground and cleaned his scrapes as best he could. They were bleeding a bit, but he seemed fine.

After James was finished, they each took a long drink of water.

"How much longer do you think?" Sigrid asked Leo. It looked to be late afternoon. The sun would be setting in a few hours.

He pulled out the map from his backpack. Sigrid and James came over to peer over his shoulders.

Leo pointed to the campsite on the map. "We're just past there." He moved his finger to the location of the Air Force base. "That's where we're heading. If we make good time, we'll probably be able to get there before the end of the day."

"If we don't have any more setbacks," James said. "There sure have been enough so far."

Back on the road, they were able to make good time. Leo and James each took turns on Sigrid's bike to tow the dog so she could get a break.

"Hey, look!" James yelled. He took a hand off the handlebar to point. Leo was trailing by a few yards but saw as he passed.

CABOT CREEK: 2 MILES

UNITED STATES AIR FORCE BASE: 11 MILES

"Oh, thank goodness," Sigrid sighed. Leo grinned. They would be there in another hour.

A few minutes later they road past a sign for the town of Cabot Creek. The town was small, split up by the highway running directly through the middle. Branching out from the highway were a convenience store, bait shop, and run-down hotel. Everything was deserted. They got off the bikes.

"Nobody here either," James said. "I wonder if they went to the base too."

Sigrid gestured to the convenience store. "We should take a look—see if there's any food or water left."

James looked uncertain about that. "Seriously? So now we're just as bad as those looters back home?"

"Well, it's not like anyone is around here waiting to buy the stuff," Sigrid said. "Besides, we've been saying this whole time that nobody knows how long the power is going to be out. Who knows the next time we'll get something to eat."

James looked over to Leo, who shrugged. "We *are* almost out of food."

"Fine," James said. "But I'm not breaking anything."

"Agreed," Sigrid said.

James took off pedaling, calling over his shoulder, "And I call dibs on any candy bars!"

Sigrid and Leo laughed as they followed after him. Finally, things seemed to be picking up for them. Leo was so excited to get something else to eat that he almost didn't notice the figure in the bait shop.

He skidded his bike to a stop. The store was dark on the inside, so all Leo could see was the outline of someone—or something—coming for them.

CHAPTER 11

All they could see was a shadow behind the light. The shadow had spindly legs and an oversized head.

"Guys!" Leo called, his body freezing up as the figure moved for the front door. "There's something in there." Sigrid and James stopped on their bikes, looking over their shoulders in the direction of the bait shop. Leo's heart pounded in his chest. But as the door slowly opened and the figure stepped out, he realized it was an older man. Leo let out a heavy breath of relief.

"Well, hello there," the man said. "Glad to see someone besides the Visitors."

"Yeah, same here," said Leo a little shakily.

"Did your town get evacuated too?"

"Not too many of us here to evacuate," the man said. "But the military did come through. I locked up and laid low."

"Why didn't you leave?"

"I ain't leavin'," he said. He gestured to the bait shop. "I've been living in the apartment above this store for thirty years now, and no Martians or soldiers are gonna take me away."

"The Visitors probably aren't from Mars," Sigrid said. The old man shrugged. It was all Mars to him, apparently.

"If you don't mind two-day-old sandwiches, I still have a few inside," the man said. "They've been in a cooler and are all right to eat. But they better get eaten soon."

"That sounds great," Leo said.

Inside, they saw that the bait shop also sold sandwiches and snacks to the fishermen who used the creek. In fact, it was a lot more than a bait shop. You could buy a rod and reel, a tent, and camping gear.

The three of them split five sandwiches between them and a pint of potato salad. Sigrid had let out Sandy, who looked thrilled to have the chance to stretch her legs. The shop owner had a few cans of dog food, and he opened one up for her. Leo offered to pay for everything, but the old man waved away the bill.

"I would have had to throw 'em out in the morning. Glad they didn't go to waste."

"Thanks for everything, um . . ." Leo said. He realized he still didn't know the man's name.

"Wendell," the old man said.

"I'm Leo. That's James and Sigrid."

"So y'all are heading for the old Air Force base then, huh?" Wendell asked around a mouthful of potato salad.

Sigrid and Leo eyed each other, still uncertain if it was wise to tell anyone else where they were going.

Wendell noticed. "Oh, come on," he barked out with a laugh. "That's where they took everyone around here. Where else would you be goin'?"

Leo cleared his throat, feeling a little embarrassed at being caught. "Uh, yeah, that's where we're going."

"Our families are there," Sigrid explained.

Wendell nodded. "Good you're going after them then."

After they finished eating, they decided it was time to keep moving. Wendell stepped outside with them to see them off.

Leo felt odd just leaving him there. "Ah, are you sure you don't want to come with us?"

Wendell grinned so widely his eyes disappeared into the wrinkles around his face. "You're nice kids. But I'll be just fine here."

They waved goodbye to him one more time before taking off pedaling. Eventually the sun began to set. Soon they spotted a side road that led to a tall wire fence and metal gate.

Leo grinned. "We made it."

***

They crept closer to the fence, hoping to get a look of the place before they approached the front gate. There were mostly soldiers in uniforms walking around. A few medics too. Deeper into the base, Leo noticed people wearing ordinary clothing.

Leo felt his stomach flip as he recognized a familiar couple. "My mom and dad are here," he said. "I think we should go in."

"Here goes nothing," James said and started toward the gate. The others joined him.

The guards spotted them approaching and stiffened, each placing a hand on their gun holster. One of the guards stepped forward. "Who are you and where are you from?"

They each gave their names. "Our families are here," Sigrid explained.

Another guard jotted down their names on a clipboard. "How come you missed the rescue vehicles?"

"I was sick so I wasn't at school," James said.

"I had to check on an . . . elderly family member," Sigrid said.

"I was out in the woods," Leo said.

One of the guards eyed the bike trailer. "What's in there?" he asked.

Sigrid's eyes went wide. "Just my dog."

The guard frowned. "Please," Sigrid said. "She's all I have. She's very well trained. She'll be good."

The guards spoke quietly with each other for a moment, and then one of them headed into the base with their names. The other guard patted them down. He looked through their backpacks and didn't take anything besides James's slingshot.

"You missed evening mess, but you can go find your families," he said.

The other guard came back for them. "All three of your families are here," he confirmed. Sigrid grinned, and James laughed in relief. "Follow me," the guard said gruffly, leading them through the large gate. They walked their bikes behind him and tried to keep up.

"Has there been any more news?" Sigrid asked. "Do we know anything more about the Visitors?"

"That information is classified," he said. Sigrid shot a concerned look over to Leo and James. The guard seemed to notice their distress. He sighed and said, "Don't worry. You'll be safe here."

But you don't know that, Leo thought as he followed. *Not really.*

The guard led them through rows of tents that were each packed with people. He checked his list and pointed them each toward the tents their families were staying in.

"Guess we're going our separate ways," said Leo after the guard walked away. He realized he didn't like the idea of being separated after all they'd been through together.

James gave a heavy yawn. He looked ready to fall asleep right then and there. Leo realized they all needed to rest and spend time with their families. "Let's meet up tomorrow after breakfast," he suggested.

Sigrid and James nodded, and the three parted to head off and find their families. As Leo wheeled his bike in the direction of his parents' tent, he found himself picking up his pace.

CHAPTER 12

Leo heard their voices before he saw them. He dropped his bike on the grass beside the tent and ducked inside.

His parents looked exhausted, with dark bags under their eyes and limp hair. Their clothes were rumpled as if they'd been wearing them for days. Given how quickly people had been evacuated, they probably *had* been wearing the same clothes for days. He'd never been so happy to see them.

"Hey," he said casually.

They looked up in surprise, and his mother's face melted into tears. "Oh, honey, I was so worried about you!" She stood up and rushed over to hug him.

His dad stepped in and hugged both of them. He was crying too. Leo realized his own eyes were a bit wet. He sniffed and wiped them on the collar.

"They said you would be on the school bus," his mother said. "What happened?"

"I wiped out on my bike. I was late to school and by the time I got there . . ."

"Never mind. You're here now!" His mom hugged him again. "You must have had quite an adventure getting here?"

"Yeah, you could say that," Leo said. "How are things here?"

"There's not enough to eat and they won't tell us anything," his dad grumbled.

"They won't even tell us when we can go home," his mother said.

Leo frowned. "So what, people are stuck here? We shouldn't need permission to leave. It's not like we're prisoners."

"No, we're not prisoners," his mother said. "But we saw a man try to leave. He said he wanted to go get his mother. The guards said he should stay for his own safety."

"Did he leave?"

His dad shook his head. "No, they talked him into staying."

"That's weird," Leo said. He didn't know how he felt about being trapped in here. What would happen if he tried to leave?

His mom seemed to sense his worry. "It might just be temporary," she said. "Until they know more about what's going on with the Visitors."

"Besides," his dad said, "leaving wouldn't be smart. We're protected here, and they're giving us food and a place to sleep. They've even managed to get some generators going."

"Dad, you said yourself, there's not *enough* food here. And no information."

"You wouldn't get any food or info out there," his dad reasoned.

"It's not too bad here," his mom said. "They said they're bringing in books and board games."

"I guess that's good." Maybe it was weird to play games while they were waiting for the Visitors to make their next move. But what else were they going to do?

"We saved you a cot," his mom said. She moved a couple of bags so he could lay down. One of the bags was his own, with fresh clothes.

A fresh change of clothes would feel great, Leo thought. He would just lie here for a moment, then get up. He stretched out on the cot and let his feet dangle off the end.

His thoughts swirled into darkness.

CHAPTER 13

"Good morning, sweetie," his mother said, shaking him gently. Leo opened his eyes and saw the sagging canvas ceiling above him. Where was he? He sat up quickly. Then he remembered. So much had happened in two days. Or was it three days? He'd lost track.

"Morning mess ends in fifteen minutes," his mom said. "Thought you might want a chance to eat."

"I do," he said.

His mother walked with him to the tables. There was a table lined with cereal, breakfast bars, and fruit. Nothing that needed to be cooked. He grabbed some dry cereal and a banana, wondering how much longer they'd have access to tropical fruit. The whole supply chain was broken. So many things he used to take for granted were gone or about to go away.

He returned to his tent to eat.

"Told you about the food," his father grumbled.

"It's not too bad," he said as he ate. "So, after breakfast I'm going to meet up with my friends."

"Steve and Joe?" his mom asked. Leo blinked, wondering for a moment who she was talking about. Then he realized she meant his friends from school. It had only been a few days since he'd seen them, but already he felt less connected to them, as if they were part of a past life. "Uh, no," he said. Maybe he would look for them after he talked to Sigrid and James. "A couple of other kids who came here with me."

"All right. Be home for lunch."

"Home?" he said, raising his eyebrows.

"You know what I mean. Meet us back here."

Leo wondered how long it would take before he thought of a cot as home. He didn't really want to find out.

Sigrid was already waiting near the spot the guard had dropped them off the day before. She'd left Sandy back at the tent so the dog could keep resting.

"Are your grandparents all right?" he asked her.

"For now," she said. "I guess. They're annoyed because nobody tells them anything."

"Same with my folks."

"Everybody's waiting for the Visitors to do something," she said.

"Yeah," he agreed. "There's nothing else to do but wait and worry."

James appeared a few minutes later.

"So what do we do today?" he asked. "I don't suppose anyone has rigged up a video game system anywhere?"

Leo and Sigrid laughed, but the truth settled in. There was nothing to do but sit around and wait. The three of them explored the grounds. There wasn't much to see. Tents and other hastily made shelters, vacated airplane hangars. Buildings locked up tight or shut off to civilians.

"You know, it wasn't easy, but I had fun the last couple of days," James said after they'd been walking around for nearly an hour.

"I was thinking that earlier," Leo said. "I felt alive. It's hard to go from that to this."

"It's like being on hold," Sigrid said.

"Waiting for an alien to pick up the phone," James joked.

The three of them laughed together, but then Leo felt their conversation take a more serious tone. "I . . . I almost wonder if it would be better out there," Sigrid said quietly.

"I've been thinking the same thing," Leo said.

"Me too," James added.

Leo nodded at them. He felt relieved to know he wasn't the only one thinking about leaving this place, that surely there were other options.

"So . . ." James scratched at the back of his head, looking from Sigrid to Leo.

"What do we do about it?"

"I'm gonna talk to my parents tonight," Leo said. "About leaving."

"Yeah. Let's all talk to our families tonight," Sigrid said. "We can meet up again tomorrow."

Sigrid and James decided to head back to their own tents. Leo stopped by to see his friends from school, but he felt restless as they played cards and chattered about everything but the Visitors. He left them and walked around some more, continuing to look around the grounds. He pretended he was just passing the time, but he was also looking for the easiest way out.

Just in case, he thought.

Dinner was strips of canned ham and bread. Apparently the army hadn't figured out how to feed this many people a hot meal yet. He ate it, wondering if he'd ever eat a hamburger and fries again. Or a piping hot pizza.

After dinner he retreated to his tent with his parents. His mother read a thick paperback, and his father fiddled with a game cube.

"What do you want to do?" his mother asked. "I have another book. It's a mystery."

Leo felt his knee rocking and his hands twitching with anxious energy. "I want to leave this place," he admitted.

"We all do, honey. I'm sure we'll go home soon."

"No, I mean now. I don't think they can force us to stay here."

"Leo, we've been over this. It's not safe to go home yet."

"Well, what if we don't go home, then? What if we go somewhere else?"

He told his parents about Wendell. "We could stay there tonight. But after that, I was thinking we could go deeper into the woods. Where no Visitors will find us."

"You wouldn't know what to do!"

"I'll learn," he told her. "*We'll* learn."

"Leo . . ." Her voice sounded so tired. "You've always been a big dreamer. Remember when you were seven and tried to start a farm in our backyard?"

His dad grabbed him by the wrist.

"Listen, Leo. This place may not be a five-star hotel, but it's safer than anywhere else. And everybody else is here."

"I know, but I can't sit still, just waiting for somebody else to tell me my fate. And if these are our last days on Earth, it seems like the worst way to spend them is being bored out of our minds. Dad, I'm going to get out of here."

"Leo, you're still a kid," his dad said, blinking in disbelief.

"But I'm not a baby."

"At least sleep on it," his mother said.

He could tell his parents weren't going to budge with this. Leo tried not to show his disappointment. "Of course."

Frustrated, he lay down on his cot, rolling away from his parents. He wished he could text his friends about his plan.

The next morning, Leo woke up early and met James and Sigrid where they had parted yesterday.

"I tried to talk my parents into leaving," Leo told them. "They didn't want to."

"My grandparents won't leave either," Sigrid said.

"My mom wants to go too, but she says she's needed here," said James.

"So what do we do?" Leo asked in a whisper.

They all looked at each other. James's eyes looked scared. Sigrid's looked determined. Leo wondered how his own looked.

"I want to go," said Leo. "At least for today. I'm going nuts."

"Me too," said Sigrid. "I'll want to come back to check on Sandy though."

"I mostly want to see if they'll *let* us leave," said James with a deep breath. They started marching toward the gate.

"What if they don't let us through?" Sigrid asked.

"I don't know," Leo whispered. "They're just doing their job. Keeping us safe. Like a lockdown, you know? I get it, but I don't know what they'll do if we insist on leaving."

The guard stepped out as they approached. He held up both hands like a traffic guard.

"For your own safety, we ask that you stay on the compound," he said.

Leo gestured to the sky beyond the fence, beyond the trees.

"We'll be right back," he said. "Just want to get a better look at that alien ship."

The guard whirled around in surprise, shielding his eyes against the sun and scanning the tops of the trees.

"Where?"

"Between the trees. Over there."

The guard squinted, scanning the sky. The other guard came and stood next to him.

"See anything? Are they here?"

They had a split second to act. Leo remembered the Death Dive—how he'd simply plunged down the hill without a second thought. If he could do that, he could do this.

"Go," he mouthed to James and Sigrid, making a shooing sign with his hand. The three of them started running.

CHAPTER 14

There were shouts behind them, but a moment later they were in the trees, ducking under branches and leaping over roots. The three of them fanned out but kept within sight of each other. After about ten minutes they came back together and stopped, heaving for air. Their heavy breaths were mixed with relieved laughter.

"I don't think they're chasing us," Leo said after he caught his breath. He searched the trees and listened carefully for noises.

"Or they haven't caught up yet," Sigrid suggested.

"You could have told us what you were going to do," James said.

"It was spur of the moment," Leo admitted. "Good thing, too. If I'd spent any time thinking about it, I would have thought of a thousand reasons it wouldn't work."

They spent the rest of the morning outside, climbing trees and exploring the woods. They found a small creek and washed their faces in the water.

"Here," Sigrid said, pulling out three granola bars from her pocket. "I swiped these at breakfast."

They sat down beside the creek as they ate the bars. Leo had to admit this felt better than being crammed into a tiny tent with everyone else.

"What now?" Sigrid asked.

"I guess we should go back to the base," said James.

"We might be in a lot of trouble," said Sigrid. "With our families and with those guards."

"I don't want to go back," Leo admitted.

"What?"

"I have this crazy idea." He took a deep and breath told them what he'd told his parents, about going deep into the wilderness and learning how to survive.

"I know it sounds really dangerous . . ." He started.

"Actually," Sigrid said quietly, "it sounds like the best idea I've heard yet."

"At least out here we get to choose for ourselves," James said. "But what about our families?"

"That's the hard part," Leo said, nodding. "Obviously I don't want to leave my parents behind. But maybe if the three of us spend a little time outside the base and then come back—if we prove we can survive out here—maybe *then* we can convince them that staying at the base is a bad idea."

"But we don't have any gear," said Sigrid.

"Or really know how to live in the wild," said James.

"Wendell's store has stuff," Leo explained. "Sleeping bags, camp stoves. Maybe he'd even come with us. I bet he knows all about living outdoors. We can do this."

As he talked a shadow fell over them.

It was too quick to be a cloud and too big to be an airplane. Not that airplanes were flying anymore.

"Don't look up," he whispered. The shadow passed. A shiver went through his body.

"It's heading toward the base," Sigrid said. Her eyes were on the grass. She didn't dare look up either. But her voice was strained with fear. Leo's thoughts flashed to his parents—his other friends—even Sandy the dog. In the same instant, he realized there was probably no way to help them. And that more than anything, their families would want *them* to find safety.

"What's gonna happen?" James asked.

"I don't know," Leo said. "But I guess now there's no going back."

ATTACK ON EARTH

WHEN ALIENS INVADE, ALL YOU CAN DO IS SURVIVE.

DESERTED

THE FALLOUT

THE FIELD TRIP

GETTING HOME

LOCKDOWN

TAKE SHELTER

LEVEL UP

WHAT WOULD YOU DO IF YOU WOKE UP IN A VIDEO GAME?

ALIEN INVASION
ISRAEL KEATS

LABYRINTH
ISRAEL KEATS

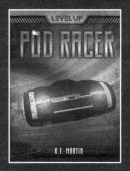

POD RACER
R.T. MARTIN

REALM OF MYSTICS
RAELYN DRAKE

SAFE ZONE
R.T. MARTIN

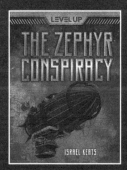

THE ZEPHYR CONSPIRACY
ISRAEL KEATS

CHECK OUT ALL THE TITLES IN THE LEVEL UP SERIES

DAY OF DISASTER

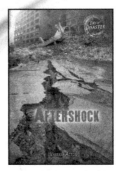

Would you survive?

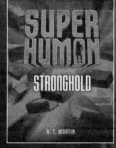

ABOUT THE AUTHOR

Israel Keats was born and raised in North
Dakota and now lives in Minneapolis. He is
fond of dogs and national parks.